MACHIEL
STONE OF THE DAMNED
A BLOOD PROPHECY NOVELLA

Barb Jones

This is a work of fiction. Names, characters, places, and incidents are products of the author's imagination or are used fictitiously and are not to be construed as real. Any resemblance to actual events, locations, organizations, or persons, living or dead, is entirely coincidental.

World Castle Publishing, LLC
Pensacola, Florida

Copyright © Barb Jones 2021
Paperback ISBN: 9781953271914
eBook ISBN: 9781953271921
First Edition World Castle Publishing, LLC, April 12, 2021
http://www.worldcastlepublishing.com

Licensing Notes

Cover: Steven J. Catizone
Editor: Maxine Bringenberg

Acknowledgement

For those that have been following the *Blood Prophecy* series, you know that these novellas are designed to bring a little more in-depth understanding of the chosen ones, who serve the prophecy in a way that brings the novels closer together. Machiel is one of the loved and hated characters, and I hope this story brings a little more compassion as to why he is the way he is. I write for my readers, and sometimes I change the story because of an idea one of you might have shared with me! So, thank you for letting me bring *Blood Prophecy* to life for you.

As for each person on the team that has helped me, whether it be Karen and Maxine from World Castle Publishing, my assistant Jessica, my cover artist Steven, my web designer Ed Bordi, and especially my kids, Arianna and Kaiden, who will be twenty and sixteen this year, THANK YOU! It was a sincere team effort, and I wouldn't be able to do it without each of you.

Enjoy *Machiel: The Stone of the Damned, and please* look forward to Zaraquel's novella. These two will help pave the way for Book Four: Rise of the Hunter.

Much love and eternal thanks,
Barb

CHAPTER 1

London, England, 1714

Machiel had just finished his red headed meal, but not completely. She was simply delicious and vivacious. As he was licking his fangs, he remembered how he had lured her into being only his consort. Kabos had taught him how to feed just enough to survive as a creature of the night, but it never satiated him. He spent months getting her to fall in love with him, and sometimes he wished he were a mortal man again. Her name was Ingrid, daughter to the only tailor in town. Ingrid was beautiful, yet she was also a powerful witch through her mother's line. He didn't know that at first, but it made him love her even more. He could taste the power in her blood. It was intoxicating, or maybe it was just that she was a willing soul to feed him. Machiel recalled the moment when her hidden truth was revealed some months prior.

They had just enjoyed a picnic dinner together, prepared by Ingrid. Politely, Machiel informed her he wasn't hungry, though he pretended to pick at the food she prepared. He wasn't ready to share his truth. But she surprised him with the fact that she already knew he was a vampire. Machiel refused her offer. He was not sure he could control himself with her yet.

"Machiel, love, you are not the only one with a secret. I am like you, but not like you. I am not a vampire, but a witch. Do you think it is by chance you found me? Fell in love with me? No, *mi amore*. I sensed you. I dreamt of you long before I met you."

Machiel felt relieved that he'd met someone like him, but not a vampire. But he was disturbed that she dreamt of him, that she knew about him. How? Machiel could not believe what he heard, but something inside him kept pulling him closer to her. It was beyond words, beyond comprehension.

Coming back to his senses, he touched her cheek, listening to her breathe. Each time he fed on her, she became more and more under his control. Kabos did teach him that certain things were against the rules of nature, like consummating with witches, killing for no reason, and engaging in the age-old custom of controlling werewolves.

Kabos was a very disciplined vampire who believed in respecting the prophecy and the way of life for a vampire. Machiel liked a challenge. After all, he was currently the most powerful vampire newborn ever made, next to Kabos. No other newborn possessed the speed, agility, or power that he had. Machiel remembered overhearing Kabos talking to another vampire about how he had never sired one quite like him. In fact, Kabos was unaware that he was listening, and Machiel heard him say things about Machiel being the one the prophecy spoke of. The training of Machiel was important, and Kabos was careful to not inflate his ego, but Machiel was so arrogant it did. The one thing Machiel could not stand anymore was the constant talk about the prophecy and how he was part of it. It was his destiny that would bring about the queen. He loathed hearing about it so much that he decided it was time to leave it behind and break the sire bond that kept him bonded to Kabos and this infuriating prophecy. He wanted to be his own vampire, to live how he wanted, answering to no one.

Ingrid began to stir and started gasping for air. Her hair was a bit disheveled, but she didn't look any worse for the wear.

"Breathe, my love. I'm sorry, but this time I took a little more so I wouldn't have to feed on you often. But I feel I must feed again, so I will go hunting later. Let's get you home to rest before your father thinks I am a mongrel. We must keep up appearances." Tenderly he touched her cheek, and her hand reached up to touch his face. She began to mumble, but he couldn't quite hear her. He leaned a little closer.

Ingrid muttered the words *"Et*

Abscondam marcam de vampyr," and her skin no longer showed the bite marks. Machiel helped her to stand, but as he did so, her eyes turned completely white and an electric shock knocked him off his feet. Machiel had never seen her eyes change like this.

Ingrid spoke once more. *"Kold en,* deathbringer. *Du forlader din skaebne ved at odelaegge lyset. Deltag med hendes lys og omfavne din skaebne."*

Machiel, versed in a multitude of languages, did not recognize this one as it was not Latin, the usual language Ingrid spoke when in a trance or while casting spells. It appeared to be much older than what he knew. Her eyes did not change, nor did she come out of her trance. Knowing his strength, he did not want to slap her to bring her back for fear that it might cause her harm. Ingrid, still tranced, began to rise in the air with her palms outward towards him. Machiel's first thought was, *Damn, not the prophecy again. Just leave me alone.*

But it did not. She spoke the same words to him again. But this time, he understood her, and he became filled with vengeance and anger. Anger consumed him, and rage filled his appetite. He looked at his beloved with hatred because to him, she was no longer Ingrid, his love. Before she could utter some additional words, his talons ripped her dress as he brought her back toward him. His fangs emerged once more, and this time, he didn't even move her hair as he tore into her neck. Because of his hearing, he could not just feel her skin, but he heard the sound of ripping flesh. Blood trickled from her as he pressed harder into her. Ingrid tried to push him away, but Machiel only held onto her tighter. He could feel the life draining from her, the witch, his love. It was as if anger consumed him.

Once there was nothing left of her blood, he threw her lifeless body to the dirt street and wiped his mouth with the remnant of her dress that was stuck to his talon. He looked down at her, took in the smell of death, and returned to the night. He loved her, but the love was replaced with his anger at the prophecy. Again, he felt like the plaything of the cursed prophecy, and he imagined the prophecy toying with him. Sometimes Machiel thought the prophecy was something of a woman's curse because of its manipulative ways in trying to get him to do something he just didn't want to do.

Ingrid's body would be found by morning light, and Machiel decided he would be long gone. He was now done with London. He would not return to

Kabos or to the house they shared—he would not. Simply would not. Machiel would prefer to ravage the cities he had not yet visited. But he must find a coffin. It would be too late to leave now. Morning would come. He would leave on the next nightfall.

"Machiel, is that you, my son? It is almost time to sleep, and I was worried the morning light would burn you. Come, now."

"Yes, Father. I am coming. But I would like to go hunting alone tonight. For practice, like you said."

"Of course, my son. But let's sleep now."

Both vampires retired to the coffins that stayed hidden in one of the many rooms upstairs. It looked like a regular bedroom, but without the traditional bed. The blue lined curtains were heavy to keep out the light and were always drawn. Candles lit the room, but only dimly. In the coffins, earth layered the bottom, and each was lined with silk that protected them. Machiel climbed in and closed the lid. As he closed his eyes, he thought briefly of the white witch and smiled at the thought of her death. For she had taken over his love's body, and he knew that Ingrid was no longer his love. Part of him relished in the mere thought of her death, but the other half mourned Ingrid. She reminded him of his past love, but she was so much more. A tear fell down his cheek as he went into a deep slumber like all vampires do.

CHAPTER 2

It was night by the time Machiel rose from the coffin. Dusk had long passed, and the quietness of the streets provided an eerie silence. While he was asleep, he was sure Ingrid's body was discovered and provided clues that would lead the townspeople to fear the predator was an animal. None of them ever imagined that a vampire existed among them. Simple mortals, coming and going with their daily lives, the only thought of something evil in the world took the form of either murder, thievery, or some other distasteful act in society.

The men were so protective of their women that they barely could recognize a vampire, a witch, or some other creature that lived among them. Even though he slept, he could just imagine the screams, the heartbeats of the women in fear, and the men trying to be brave, but really weren't. Looking at Kabos's coffin, he could see it was already empty. His father must have gone out.

Machiel had not slept well. Killing his love did not satisfy him. Instead, he was plagued with thoughts of another, but he couldn't make out the details. But the thoughts were not of a woman — lust did not consume him. It was as if he were another vampire, and through his eyes, he watched as a female vampire and her mate kissed with passion and fervor. Machiel could feel his anger rise and then disappear. Another thought of being bound and tortured by a mere woman, causing his blood to boil. He knew that was impossible, but he recalled the feeling because he hadn't been a vampire for long. In fact, Kabos and others referred to him as "newborn." Newborns were not able to control their strength, rage, and many other things properly, but the one thing that made Machiel stand out from previous newborns from Kabos was his inexplicable sense of feeling his humanity from before. That just did not disappear. He recalled Kabos saying that perhaps one day it might serve his destiny and a higher purpose. There were nights when they went hunting that Kabos even spoke to him about the possibility that Machiel was not just a newborn but one of the ancient vampires who just returns to life after life. He didn't believe in such tales, but there were so many times he had the strangest dreams and couldn't make sense of it all.

Instead of sitting there daydreaming, Machiel packed a few belongings into a satchel and closed the door behind him. In his head, he heard a woman's voice. *Machiel, you can't forsake the prophecy. You need Kabos. You need to learn. Find the one whose blood will come from you and others. Find her. Seek her.*

Machiel growled. He had no interest in the prophecy or some crazy notion of finding some girl. He did not want to be a maker or be responsible for anyone other than himself. Machiel didn't want to get married to the cow his father had chosen for him, and he most certainly did not want it the night he left with Kabos. In fact, that's why he slept with his father's serving girls and more. But it was Rosalia, the favorite serving girl in his father's house, that always fascinated him. Breathing a sigh, he knew that was the past. That's why, when he met Ingrid, he felt he had the power of control in his life as a vampire. His father was not there. In fact, he controlled his destiny with Ingrid, at least up until he killed her.

Machiel walked the night. The streets were empty. As he rounded the corner at the far end of the street, he heard two men talking in the distance. Practicing his honing skills, he cocked his head a little and picked up the conversation. As he eavesdropped on their conversation, he just smiled at how quick thinking he had been to cover up a vampire attack.

"They think it was a wild wolf or some dog. Perhaps it was tame, but his master didn't feed it. I heard them say the animal practically ripped out her throat."

"Who was it? The poor girl."

"It was Ingrid, the daughter of the

tailor. Her father is beside himself. First, his wife and baby died in childbirth, leaving Ingrid and him all alone. They say his wife was a kindhearted woman, but her body was so weak from childbirth. Ingrid was his only joy since then. And now he is all alone in this world."

"She was a good girl. But wasn't she seeing a young man, the new one in town? Michael or Matthew or something?"

"Yes. From what I hear, she was beginning to love him, and her father would have blessed the union if the young man felt the same way. He will be distraught. But I know he is busy during the day, that he might not have heard the news yet. He usually roams the streets at night, the young lad. But my wife will be making him and Ingrid's father something to help ease their loss. Sustenance is important during this time. Perhaps we will see the young man and tell him."

"I suppose you're right. Maybe the lad will even take to helping her father through this ordeal. I believe I spoke to him once, and he was so polite."

Machiel couldn't walk in that direction anymore. He didn't want to stop and hear the condolences. He simply wanted to hunt and run away. He turned and decided to use the rooftops instead. Forget the streets.

Machiel used his speed and agility to get out of town faster than he normally would when he went hunting. At the last rooftop, he sat perched and peered over his shoulder for one last look. Running his hand through his blond hair, he paused for a moment to practice listening, but instead, he heard the same voice as the one that had spoken through Ingrid. Was it her ghost? No, Machiel didn't believe in such foolishness. But then again, anything was possible.

"*Child of the Chosen Ones. You seek what you cannot yet see. You hunt for what you crave but cannot catch. Through the light, through the darkness, you will face a foe unlike any other. From the past, he will come and seek you. Two halves you are, a whole you will make. Through your vengeance will come her blood. But first, love will be in your heart, my son. If you leave the fold now, he will find you and give you rebirth to the darkness.*"

Machiel let out a scream before leaving the town. His scream filled the silence of the night air. The night began to turn cold once he made his decision to turn his back on the prophecy and his father to head into a new world. Lightning struck, and a loud crash filled the night sky. The moon that had shone brightly now turned black, and the air changed. The prophecy heard this and spoke in its own way once more to him. Machiel could hear the rumblings from the prophecy and chose not to tell Kabos, as it would only entice the foolish vampire to believe more firmly that Machiel was the one to set the path in motion. Machiel was firm in his decision and thought, just for a second, that maybe there was some truth to what Kabos had been saying all along. But why him? He was nothing special before he was a vampire. Simply a rich son with a strong lust for women.

"Child, you forsake the prophecy with this. Therefore, your path has changed. I curse you to the unknown, and he will find you. Your destiny will haunt you with the blood you will drink. No more will you drink from humans, but of the animals lesser than you. The blood of man will burn you, but the blood of rats will sustain you. This curse will last until you meet the white wolf and the white witch once more. You will be nothing

more than an animal until you return to your ways of the prophecy. Into the darkness you go to return to the light."

CHAPTER 3

It had been months since he left, and Machiel was no better than a mongrel that roamed endlessly. He tested the prophecy that had spoken her curse and tried to feed on a woman. The blood he drank burned in his veins, and his flesh began to darken with the scent of death. Blisters formed on his skin, and he threw her to the side and searched for something else to eat. She was still breathing but lay unconscious. He looked at the woman and felt nothing for her. Despite what the curse could unleash against him, he still could smell her blood. In his mind, he was hungry, but the burning sensation stopped him. His flesh continued to blister as her blood coursed through him from the little he had managed to drink. This was a worse feeling than the blood rage that vampires endured. The pain was more than he could stand. He wanted to die. Death must be better than what his body was feeling. Machiel heaved until there was nothing more of her in him. From that moment on, he believed he was cursed. He fed on the animals that roamed.

Still sensing a connection to Kabos, Machiel fought the urge to be found by his father. In some ways, he wanted to be found, rescued, but in others, he remained defiant. Machiel wandered through new towns. He found himself in Italy, leaving England behind, working at the docks. It was easy work considering his strength and the fact that he preferred to work at night while the crew slept. It made it easier to feed on rats and other filthy animals. He worked from the minute the sun went down to early dawn, being careful not to attract attention to his state. At one point in his life, he was considered a handsome man, with looks that attracted women of all ages and lifestyles to him. But now, he hadn't shaved in so long, his stubbles formed into a blond beard, and his eyes looked like he was a beaten man, with no direction in life. This made him all the more easy to hire and not have the captain raise any questions.

"Boy, come here," said the captain. "I need you to mop the deck and empty the buckets. We set sail three days from now. You are strong. I could use you at sea. What do you say?"

In his short time as a vampire, he had managed to keep his secret hidden, but this would be different. There was no way he would be able to conceal his true nature while in the middle of the sea. But he felt worthy for the first time in his life. Before being bitten, his real father did not appreciate him, so he had turned his attention to whoring with the servant girls. Sighing, he said, "Captain, I can't. But I am happy to keep working till you set sail. I will be here should you return. I just have too many other side obligations I must fulfill."

The captain chuckled and slapped him on the back. "Damn women. They always take the good ones." The captain turned around and walked back towards his ship.

Machiel finished the orders and decided to walk the dock. He felt a stirring sensation from his belly and a sudden pain. It made him double over, and he glanced at his surroundings. He didn't feel like he was staked or anything. Looking down at his hands and patting himself everywhere, he found that everything was still intact. But the pain was intense, and as he fell to his knees, he covered his ears and let out a piercing scream. He knew that if he kept up the screaming, someone would hear. It wasn't hunger, though he missed the blood of women. It was something more, something more sinister and violent. In fact, it brought his body an extreme amount of pain though nothing physically was harming him.

Standing upright once more, Machiel continued on his way. This time, another pain was coursing through him, but he didn't falter, though he no longer could see what was in front of him.

Visions clouded his mind, like scenes from the past. He saw a man burning one of his kind. This man had a mark on his cheek, and a hat pulled down to hide his eyes. Then he saw a demon or something like that. In his hand was a cup, an ordinary cup. Scenes of burning vampires filled his mind to the point where he felt like he could smell the stench. It made his stomach turn. Machiel then saw what he thought was the white witch, only because the figure was silvery white. But it wasn't Ingrid or any other woman he knew. It was a dark-haired woman dressed all in white. Her skin was fair, and she had the reddest lips he had ever seen. Her bodice enticed his body, but her finger raised and pointed as if she was standing right in front of him. Another electric pain shot through his body. He could feel his body come alive with the flick of her finger. But was she real? He no longer could tell what was real or what was not. The intensity was becoming too much to bear.

A man approached him from the side. Machiel couldn't see any more than the outline of a hand that reached for him. Blinded with such agonizing pain, Machiel was not the hunter he usually was. In fact, he was caught so completely off guard that he did not recognize the man or his scent. But, like an animal in fear, Machiel's fangs emerged, nostrils flared. The man raised his hand that held a crucifix. The brim of the man's hat covered his face, leaving only a shadow and a mark on his cheek that was not easily seen. Recalling his visions, Machiel thought this man looked vaguely familiar. But there was no way Machiel could have premonitions or anything like that. So how could this man be familiar to him?

"Beast, stay down. Do you not know who I am?"

The man started to mumble some inaudible sayings, but Machiel could tell they were not pleasant things. Machiel strained to listen to what he was saying, considering the pain was so unbearable and excruciating.

"Foolish vampire. These spawns of hell are like poisonous vipers to mortals. Lucky for me, they brought me a new purpose in life to get my Mary back. All I have to do is kill each and every vampire to destroy the prophecy and send these creatures back to Hell."

Machiel couldn't move. The crucifix paralyzed him, and for the first time as a vampire, fear set in. Machiel closed his eyes and cowered at this man's feet. Then it was a miracle. He could move again. Looking up at the man, he definitely recognized him. It was the man from his visions. And Machiel knew the mark on his cheek. The mark of the vampire. He knew about this hunter because Kabos had made sure Machiel knew his history of vampires and that they are not evil creatures, just different — with a different purpose.

"I am Valentine. You, my boy, are the one I seek. Oh, I won't kill you. At least not yet. Instead, I am going to humble you before God. Then we will talk."

Hands pulled Machiel up, and he could feel himself being thrown over the side of a horse. Still weakened by the crucifix, he was in no position to fight back yet. To keep him immobile, the man placed the crucifix close enough to Machiel so they could travel.

It must have been hours later that Machiel woke with a start, followed by immense pain. Finding himself tied to a chair, he started screaming. He didn't know why he was screaming, as he was still groggy, but as he regained more of his senses, he knew something was happening, and it wasn't in a good way. Pain filled his body once more, but he couldn't remember from what. He tried to reach out for Kabos, but his mind was not lucid. Focusing his eyes, he saw his arm, full of needle holes. The smell of burning flesh filled his nose once more. The searing pain was so much that Machiel passed out once more.

Valentine slapped him across the cheek. Machiel didn't feel as lucid as before, but he knew something was wrong. It wasn't night yet, that much he could sense. His body was tired, and he smelled like burnt flesh. Focusing on his sense of smell first, he tried to smell his surroundings. He could smell dry goods and lots of sawdust. When he could smell nothing more, he opened his eyes fully and glanced around. Right in front of him stood the man, the hunter, the one Kabos had told him about. In one hand, Valentine held onto the crucifix, and in the other, a glass vial. The crucifix touched Machiel's chest, branding its shape right above his pectoral muscle. Valentine pushed it hard into his chest to really make its impression and then used the vial to pour the holy water on it. The searing flesh made it possible to bring Machiel fully awake and aware of his predicament.

Screaming from the torture, Machiel finally spoke. "Foolish hunter. Whom do you seek? Tell me so I can search the boy's memories for the one you seek." Valentine did not answer. Again, Machiel's voice spoke, even louder than the first time. "Hunter of the prophecy's children. You have summoned me when it is not time. Whom do you seek? Is it Mary? She lives in the world of the damned. Is it the wolf? The witch? Or is it the one true queen that you seek?"

Machiel could hear himself speak, but he did not understand, nor did he care. All he wanted at this point was to either die or be saved so he could drain this fool man. He did not care if the curse would kill him. He wanted the death of the hunter.

CHAPTER 4

Machiel glanced around once more, taking in his surroundings. He decided to allow himself to be "humbled" by the hunter to regain his strength. They were in a storeroom of some kind. The windows were covered, but his body told him it was daylight. The hunter paced back and forth beside the table that held sacred relics of some kind. Machiel honed his hearing and to understand the mutterings of the hunter. He focused his eyes to look more closely at the table with the relics. He noticed that they looked very aged but couldn't quite make out what they were. Machiel then realized that these looked similar to the relics Kabos always had hidden away and moved with them whenever they went to a new place.

"Why won't he come? It is him I need to speak to. Not this vampire boy."

Then Machiel saw something on the table that caught his eye, something covered in a red cloth, tied with a rope. Next to it lay some books Machiel. Focusing on the pages of the one book that lay open, he saw the words "prophecy, witch, wolf, vampire, cursed in blood, moon." There was more. It looked like a story, a legend or something. Machiel cursed under his breath. There was no turning away from this cursed prophecy.

The hunter returned and loosened Machiel's ropes. Machiel started to feel stronger once more. At least the hunter didn't drug him again. Instead, the hunter threw him a sword. Machiel's right hand caught the hilt of the sword. The blade began to glow. It was as if the sword was made for him. Preposterous!

Machiel stood on his feet and began to swing the sword in arc circles, allowing the blade to become one with him. Machiel raised the sword high and brought it down in a fast sweeping motion, followed by quick movement with his feet, while the sword eventually remained pointed toward the hunter. The hunter started laughing because, in that instant, the sword began to burn Machiel's flesh. "Damn. Not again." This time, however, the sword would not leave his hand. In fact, the hand and the sword became one. Machiel could not make a single move that would force his hand to release the sword. Instead, his hand gripped the sword even tighter than before, causing him to wince at the power the sword had over his hand.

Valentine approached him again. This time he called for the sword, and Machiel's hand released its grip. Machiel and Valentine danced in a circle, both teasing each other for a fight. But instead, Valentine stopped and called to him in an ancient language.

"*Du te, Du te, Cometh hitu hitu.*"

Machiel convulsed and lost consciousness.

Something came out of Machiel's mind like he was seeing things happening but was no longer in control of anything. He just witnessed the next moments. He was a silent observer, and that he did not like.

"Hunter. You summon me. Is she here? Is my queen here, that wretched whore? Have you found me a host?"

Machiel quivered inside his consciousness. He could only witness this, but he needed Kabos more than ever. What was it the voice of the prophecy had said? He needed to meet a white wolf and a white witch. He wished he could change this whole thing forever. Reaching deep inside his being, he realized if he was this chosen boy or something, he must have some kind of power they all wanted. What was it? Why him?

He could see Valentine reach for an instrument with a sharp blade. He held it in his hands as he circled Machiel. Again, the two of them spoke.

"You are the king, are you not?" asked the hunter.

"It is I. The one created from the First One. The first blood drinker."

"I give you my service to eradicate your kind, leaving only the ones that truly serve the darkness and the First One. Is it true that she is your consort right now? In exchange for my service, I ask only one thing. Bring back my Mary, my sweet Mary."

Machiel, or the husk of Machiel, extended his hand towards the hunter. Machiel could see that the hunter was not sure yet if it was him or the so-called king that the hunter had summoned. What caught Machiel by surprise was that somehow his body had merged with the king, but he was still in there as well. The two were "trapped" together in Machiel's body. Both gripped each other and shook. Machiel could feel him laughing at the hunter, but the bargain was struck. An agreement was made. Again, lightning pierced the sky because a promise to work together was made, and Machiel felt this promise would last a lifetime — or many lifetimes, considering he was immortal. Machiel could feel his insides twist in terror as he listened to them both talk about prophecies, dead queens, vampire killings. And then the most important words were heard — the white witch. The most powerful witch in favor of the Chosen Ones. The one who would silently guide the prophecy's children to their destiny. Machiel remained silent so he could hear about this white witch.

Still silent inside his own body, Machiel wanted to scream but couldn't. He wanted to claw his way to freedom but couldn't. Instead, he was at the mercy of the imaginary king in his body and this hunter. He was so afraid his thoughts would be heard by the so called king that he tried to think of idiotic things that meant nothing. He thought of ale, women, rats that he feasted on. He knew he was hungry, and it had been so long since he fed off a mortal that tasted rich in blood compared to disease infected rats. Then he heard the voice again, speaking to him.

"Foolish boy, you think I won't hear you because the hunter does not? Let me show you who I am. I am the king, the one that made so many like you. I am the one that haunts dreams of newborns as makers try to teach you the way of life because not only have I made vampires, I have even killed them. In fact, I killed my own maker, my mother. So do not think for a moment that you can fool me because you can't. I am you. You are me. We are one, and when this stupid hunter finishes what he needs to do, you will be with me as long as you do not get yourself killed."

"Listen to me, hunter man, and listen closely. Only the white witch could bring your Mary back. She is the true guardian of the prophecy. No one can destroy her, but perhaps you can find a way to alter the prophecy to suit the Tall Dark Man and his ultimate plan. Seek her through the child of this foolish vampire you hold hostage. She is called by many names, but innocence is worn on her face because she is a child and an old woman all at the same time. She can change her appearance. The white witch will either guide this vampire or turn him from it. I can hear him still inside me, but his voice is becoming distant. He thinks to best me at his game, but I have subdued him with my words. He will not raise a finger against me. The longer he resists the prophecy's hold, the weaker he will be to control if he is the host. But you must insert the stone of the damned into his body. If he survives its hold and power, then he is the one we need. Eventually, the white witch will find him, but hopefully, it will be too late by then. Do you have the stone?"

"Yes, I brought it with me from one of the last hunts I did. It was not easy because a fool left it guarded by werewolves. But I eliminated the filthy dogs. If I serve you and the master — er, The Tall Dark Man or whatever — I want my Mary. Otherwise, go find another hunter to be your mongrel fool and do your bidding. I will not wait centuries, I tell you. Bring me my Mary now, or else I will flame the vampire, and you have no host."

Valentine shook his head in defiance towards the prophecy and this king. But there was a change in Machiel. He could feel it. It was like the king released some of the hold he had on Machiel, allowing him to have a little control over his body, but not much. Machiel shook hands with Valentine. The two struck a deal, and the gentleman's handshake bonded them. To seal the deal, Valentine took the item that lay in the red cloth and unwrapped it. In it was a scroll and what appeared to be an ancient relic. Machiel looked closer at it by really focusing his sight on it. It looked like a puzzle box. He continued to stay silent while the "guest" remained in control of his body.

Valentine opened the box and pulled out a simple blade. He read from the parchment, and the blade turned red. He ripped open Machiel's shirt further and found the point where his ribs met his belly and started to cut. Machiel screamed — though he was a vampire, he could still feel pain. As he screamed, the king inside him laughed uncontrollably, as if he enjoyed the torment Machiel was experiencing. From the box, Valentine also pulled out a stone. He held the stone high enough to ensure that Machiel would see it, which meant the king would see it.

Valentine said, "If you two exist together when this is all done, which will you be? The king or still the vampire?"

Machiel found his voice, though it

was the king who spoke. "If the boy is the true host that I need, then the boy will be nothing but a shell, and I will have risen once more."

He inserted the stone into Machiel's core, and before long, Machiel healed himself.

Valentine called out once more to Machiel. "Is it you, boy, or the king?"

"It is still me, Alaric. The king that you now serve. In turn, I serve the master. The Tall Dark Man. We are not done, Hunter. If this fool vampire lives and is the one, then he will be the host. Remember our agreement. Remember that it will always be me whenever you see this boy. It will never be this vampire again, so you can not kill him, or you will kill me. Serve the master by serving me, and you will have your pitiful Mary again. As agreed. Defy me, Hunter, and I will torment Mary with no end in sight.

Her soul is sweet, and even with all the torture she has endured, she remains pure to you. She continues to pray for your soul and still loves you. Filthy. Disgusting. But you must kill the ones who will not be loyal to me or to the master. Harm this boy more for pleasure and practice, but do not kill him. I need him to be the host. I sense his strength finally. He has been toying with us by pretending to be silent and weak. Do not underestimate this one. He has been taught well by his maker, despite how young he is."

With that, Machiel could feel the presence leaving his body and felt the stone in his body. It clung to his insides, and somehow this stone made sure Machiel knew it was alive inside him. His stomach hurt, but then it dissipated till he no longer felt it. Moments later, Machiel felt it again and then it subsided. First, the king toyed with his mind and body, and now this stone taunted him with such power. Machiel could feel its hold, and no matter how much he tightened his core, the stone was alive inside him.

Valentine laughed again at Machiel's plight and continued his torture of him. Machiel was the victim to this cruel hunter, but in silence, he vowed his revenge. Burned in daylight, burned in holy water, burned by the crucifix, there was not a spot left on Machiel that wasn't touched by the hunter. In fact, his body belonged to the hunter through this torture. If he cried out in pain, the hunter only laughed. If he endured in silence, the hunter only grew angrier. Machiel decided enough was enough. Calling upon his inner voice, remembering what Kabos had taught him—that he was the one the prophecy spoke of—he called upon the prophecy herself. He willingly succumbed to her servitude. He was done rebelling for the moment.

Moments later, he felt a power unlike any other he had felt. It couldn't remove the strange feeling he felt in his abdomen from the stone, but it gave him a sense of power and strength. He basked in it as he pretended to be weakened by the torturous acts.

By nightfall, the hunter gathered up Machiel and threw him back to the docks, where he would either be found or would rescue himself. Machiel thought to himself that the hunter would pay one day, either with his life or with his Mary. Who was Mary? Another one of the prophecy's mysteries. He was going to get his revenge one way or another. It mattered not if he was going to just be a "shell," as the king called it, he promised to kill the hunter regardless, and he would. It was just a matter of time.

CHAPTER 5

Machiel healed from the ordeal with the hunter, stronger than before, renewed, with a sense of purpose and destiny. Through this, he could feel Kabos again. On some nights, he felt horrid for what he had done. Other nights, he was just lonely. But one thing was for certain — his appetite for blood was changing. He was no longer feeding off the rats in the gutters. He decided to try for a human again. Imagining the sweet flavor of her blood made his fangs protrude. Machiel decided to try his hand at hunting once more. Before he went hunting, he checked out his other abilities and found they were different from before. He was faster, his eyesight was better, his talons were longer than before. In fact, he felt more carnal than before. He could sense that his "humanity" side, the side that Kabos kept nurturing in him, was slowly disappearing. *What kind of vampire was this king? He must have been a brutal sort.* But before he could continue his thoughts, he went hunting. Machiel wanted to put his improved skills to the test.

He came across a woman, all by herself, just leisurely walking the streets. Before, he would always play with his food, teasing them, flirting with them, but he did not feel the need to do so. Taking her by surprise, he drained her completely. He couldn't resist because the temptation was too great, and nothing tasted sweeter than her blood. After his dinner, Machiel continued his roaming of the night till he came upon the house most familiar to him.

In the shadows, he stood in front of his father's house. He saw his mother, sister, and eventually his father. And then there she was — Rosalia, the French serving girl in his father's employment. She was still as beautiful as ever, but something about her was different. A small child ran around her mother's skirts, and there was something familiar about her. The girl looked in Machiel's direction, and he hid in the shadows. It was night, and he knew enough about children to know that normally they were in bed at this time, but it looked like Rosalia was still working for his father. He couldn't have expected Rosalia to leave his father's employ because he was gone. She was a loved member of his former family.

Machiel continued to watch

them. His father approached the small child. Machiel listened once more on a conversation.

"How is my sweet little angel tonight? Did you get dessert for being such a lovely child?"

"Yes, Grandfather. Can I ask you something? Do you see the man over there? He's hiding. Do you know him?"

"I don't see anyone, child. Can you show me where? Or is this one of your games that you like to play? I will play if you like."

The little girl took her grandfather's hand and began walking toward Machiel. Machiel did not want to be seen, but there was something about this little girl that kept him where he stood. He tried to hide in the shadows. It wasn't that he didn't try to leave because he did. But he couldn't move. Something powerful kept him in place. But it was not the king. He didn't think it was the stone — or was it?

Then he saw her eyes — they were white. She had blonde hair, like him, and a cute pixie-like nose, with rosy cheeks. Machiel used his senses to really look at her. Her face reminded him of his mother and sister. But she also looked like a miniature Rosalia. It couldn't be. Not his child. But then again, he'd had Rosalia so many times before becoming a vampire. So maybe. Could this be what the king mentioned?

"Sweet child, I don't see anyone. But how do you know someone is there without your sight?"

"Because I can feel him, Grandfather. I can feel him. He's over there." And she pointed to exactly where Machiel stood. But his father could not see him well enough.

Machiel looked at Rosalia. Her breasts were firm, and her small waist still intact. Obviously, child birthing had no effect on her. She was still as intoxicating as he remembered, and a blood tear flowed down his cheek. The stone burned his stomach again, and Machiel winced at the pain. Then he noticed the child clutch her stomach and whisper, "The pain will go away if you learn to control it."

Machiel noticed from afar his father's disposition. The years had not hurt him, as he still looked fit as a fiddle. He obviously loved his granddaughter, but did he miss his son? It appeared to be the case. Machiel's mother scooped up the little girl in her arms to bring her into the house, but she smiled and waved in Machiel's direction.

Leaning against the tree, Machiel cried a little more. He knew that leaving his father's house that night would cause some pain, especially with the wedding that would have united his house and Lysbette's family into one. Again, all about a business transaction.

Rosalia looked in the direction her daughter kept pointing at. Machiel could see that Rosalia was aware of something. Hoisting up her skirts, she made her way towards Machiel. He didn't hear her approach.

She gave a startled scream. Machiel looked at her and made his eyes downcast.

"Don't look at me, Rosalia. But it is me, Mach."

"Mon Dieu, is it really you? After all this time? You are pale, Machiel."

"It is me, Rosalia. How do you fare, my sweet?"

"Very well. I have a daughter now. Your parents are still kind to me and to her."

"Rosalia, is she mine? Do you know

what I am now?"

Rosalia lowered her head as if she were ashamed to say the words. "Yes, she is yours. You disappeared that night before I could tell you, but you had other things on your mind, Machiel. But she is not a normal child. She has something about her that makes her different. However, in a lot of ways, she is you. I guess that's why your father has such joy when he is with her. Let's go tell them you have come home."

Machiel shook his head in disagreement. He reached for her hand.

Rosalia pulled away. "It is cold, Machiel. You are cold."

"No, Rosalia. I am dead. I live among the night now. But is my daughter like me?"

Rosalia was still afraid but not that afraid of Machiel. "No, she is blind. Her eyes are white, but she does the strangest things. She sometimes mutters in a different language about things we do not understand. But you should meet her, Machiel. She is yours. I am not married."

Rosalia invited Machiel back into the house, but he came in secretly. She escorted him back to his old room, which was now hers and her daughter's. Rosalia explained to him that she needn't work anymore, but she happily did so for his father. They welcomed her into the family, knowing that she carried Machiel's child and that he, technically, had disappeared from their lives.

"Tell me about her, Rosalia. Tell me about my daughter. I never thought I would have this chance after I left."

"Sit. Listen. It was strange after you left. The marriage was called off when you disappeared. Lysbette was broken-hearted, and her father returned the dowry that he was paid—minus a portion, of course. That infuriated your father, but he agreed that it was more than fair since he would have to find another husband for that girl. That dowry became your daughter's dowry for when the time comes for her to marry. Your mother insisted that I agree so she can have opportunities at a nice life. The birth was an easy one, but once she was here, strange things always happened. She spoke one time about a girl named Diana and a parchment that would find its way to you in years to come. Then she spoke of a man named Kabos, whoever that is. But my favorite story she likes to tell is the one of a man, I assume you, who would find his queen. It was like listening to strange stories. But just last night, she screamed. She said that a man will come who will bend her to his power, to enslave her for a dark man. Machiel, I am afraid. These stories…. Well, some are like children's fairy tales, but the others seem wicked. What are you, my love?"

Machiel faced her and let the blood tears flow. He opened his shirt and showed her the burn marks. Not all his marks had disappeared. He was healed, but the imprints remained on his skin, probably as a self-serving reminder.

With a heavy sigh, he told her about all things sacred to vampires and how he came to be before he left that night, leaving all behind him when Kabos rescued him. He actually felt relieved having shared his thoughts and secrets with the one person, next to Kabos, of course, that he really cared about. It wasn't that he didn't care about his family because he did, but they never really understood him. Rosalia nodded as if she understood and moved her hair away from her neck, giving him permission to drink from her. Machiel couldn't. He told her why. He told her about Ingrid, whom he did love as well, but ended up killing her. Machiel could not do that to his sweet Rosalia. Rosalia was the world to him, and now, this little girl was part of his world.

Machiel listened as Rosalia told him a little more about her past, about things he didn't bother getting to know when he was with her. Back then, he only had one thing on his mind with her, and it certainly was not to get to know her past. Rosalia was part gypsy. Through her mother, she carried the gypsy blood, but her father was a horseman that came across their caravan one day. He stayed, but only until she was born. Then her mother's people told him to leave for the safety of the baby. For Rosalia. Brokenhearted, her father left her mother's people. Rosalia grew in the ways of the sight and foretelling. She made sure that Machiel understood their daughter carried this power within her. That this was possibly what made her different.

CHAPTER 6

The bedroom door opened, and in came their little girl. Finally, Machiel had the courage to ask, "What is your name, child?"

"Beatrix. I know you. You are the one they seek. You are the one that the prophecy needs."

Rosalia introduced Beatrix to Machiel. Beatrix held out her hand. Machiel caught a whiff of her scent, her blood. The smell was different from Rosalia, so different that Machiel took a deeper inhale to catch her scent. In fact, his child's blood was calling to him. It was like Beatrix's blood was singing to him, but only he could hear it.

"You seek the white witch, and maybe the white wolf too. I don't know. But I know you want to find the white witch. What is it you seek, Father?"

Rosalia and Machiel looked at each other, each as perplexed as the other. Finally, Machiel broke the silence and spoke to his daughter. "Are you the white witch?"

Beatrix remained silent. Her eyes began to flutter. A soft song came through her lips. Machiel stared in amazement at this child. His child.

"Machiel sired son of the believer. I am the white witch you seek. I feel your power. Your strength. Your desires and curses. Listen to me closely. Mark the words you will hear from this sweet child.

"The hunter has you in his grasp.

The stone of the damned is inside you. The prophecy cannot protect you until you remove it. If you don't remove it, it will continue to feed on you little by little. Find the white wolf in a cave between two worlds. You will know this cave because of the rivers that connect it. One stream flows up while the other flows down. The wolf will know you and will know what to do. You had the taste of freedom from the prophecy and suffered its punishment for turning your back on her, but she gives you the power you need to sustain you till you find the white wolf. Drink from this child, your child. Be connected even more and find what you seek. But hurry. The hunter comes for this child. She must be cloaked once you drink from her. Drink, Machiel. Drink."

Machiel hung his head in solace and realized that drinking from this child was going to be hard. But there was little to no choice in the matter. He was the one to make a queen, the one to find a witch and wolf, to be a host, to be more than he seemed. He never asked for this, but he felt a sense of duty now, pride to be part of something much bigger than him. The child came closer to Machiel and hugged him. Machiel felt a power from her that he had never felt before. It radiated through his being and provided him with a sense of courage.

He separated himself from her to look at her. Then he saw it. Her eyes. They were the exact same as Ingrid's. *Oh God, what have I become? Must I really drink from my own child?*

Again, Beatrix spoke to him. "Father, Chosen One. You are more than what you seem. Courage, vengeance, destiny, love, truth are all part of who you are. But you are an ancient soul. You have been given many lives, just like the one who will be your true destiny. To find her, you must be all these lives. Return to Kabos. Find the white wolf. But before you leave this place, remember the stone inside you. It will kill you if you wait too long. Drink from the prophecy. Drink from me. What you will drink will keep the stone dormant until you find the white wolf. But seek forgiveness from your father, Kabos, and he will aid you."

Rosalia and Machiel looked at their daughter, but she didn't sound like their daughter. Rosalia was beginning to look really frightened, and Machiel kissed her. "I have always loved you."

And with that, he took Beatrix's wrist and began to drink. Her blood did not taste like blood at all. It was sweeter than human blood. It wasn't even red. Somehow, whatever it was, Machiel needed it most. The stone must have felt the power he was drinking, and it started to react. It was like a battle in the pit of his stomach, but soon the stone became silent. He continued to drink, pressing harder into little Beatrix's wrist. Rosalia pushed Machiel away after a bit, and then he saw it. Beatrix's eyes became normal. Normal blue eyes.

"You did it. Machiel, continue your path. Seek the next one. Return to Kabos, your — maker. Seek what you must. Before you return to Kabos, listen closely once more. You will have questions, but those answers will come in time. The prophecy will send you those that will stand by you in ways you cannot imagine, so do not turn them away. The prophecy has always watched out for you, Machiel, so learn from your mistakes and forge your destiny with the queen. But a day will come that will test your heart and mind. It is written in the stars."

That was not the last time Beatrix spoke in strangeness about the prophecy. But Machiel didn't leave right away. He wanted to get to know his daughter, and they talked until his father walked in and fainted at the sight of his son.

"Go, Machiel. Go before he comes to. His heart can't take another loss, and with you being what you are now, this will kill him for sure. Come see us when you can in this lifetime. If you can't, I will understand, and my heart will always belong to you. But live for the prophecy and do what is asked of you. Fulfill your destiny, my love."

Machiel embraced them both and left through the same window he had done years before. He couldn't believe it. He had a daughter. And it felt so good to see Rosalia. And somehow, the prophecy used her to speak to him.

Machiel decided to remain in

Bruges for a few more nights. He was always nearby where Beatrix could sense him, and she always smiled in his direction. Somehow she managed to let Rosalia know, and she would glance around. Never seeing Machiel, though, she just smiled so he could see how much she truly loved him. Once he was confident the hunter was not coming for them, he set afoot to find Kabos. It was time to start his quest, but not until he connected once more with Kabos, perhaps to beg for forgiveness.

CHAPTER 7

Machiel returned home to Kabos. The old man was joyous to see him based on the embrace he received.

"My son. You have come back to me. I'm guessing there's something of great urgency that you must do. Tell me, my son. Tell me all from the beginning."

Machiel, a fully healed vampire, fell to his father's feet and begged for mercy. "I don't know, Father. I couldn't take it anymore. I don't want to be the one to make the queen or fulfill some crazy story, but no matter what I do, I can't escape it. I think perhaps I wanted to be free for just a little bit, and I know you believe fully in this prophecy stuff, but it's a bit scary at times. I mean, to unite ourselves with other races that are beneath us? It's not quite normal. At least not to me. We are vampires. We are supposed to be the supreme race. We can live among the humans, and those werewolves are meant to serve us. They deserve to be in chains. I met some kind of hunter. He knew how to break me, and then he had this king inside me, giving him orders like he commanded the hunter. And he eventually did. Father, I just don't know what to believe in anymore. I miss the days of my sweet Rosalia. I…I…. Never mind."

"Son, let me tell you something I have not yet shared. When I was a young one, my mother had a special gift and a bloodline so powerful the fates chose my path for me. Unlike you, I had no choice but to answer its call. My mother, blessed be that woman, was a gypsy from the oldest populations ever known. She was a Romani gypsy, and my father was not. I was born of a union that should never have been allowed, but who can stop love?"

He noticed that the old man grew silent, somber, as if he was remembering his parents. *I wonder how long he has been alone.*

"Ah, Machiel. I digress. Fates told my mother I had been called by the stars to do something. I have what you call the mark of the gypsy. I am the keeper of the gypsy prophecy, and that, my boy, is intertwined with it all. Each race has a prophecy — the witches, the werewolves, the vampires, the gypsies, and I'm sure countless others. What the races do not seem to fathom is the mere idea of working together, being bound together as one. I guess you could say the only ones that can conceive of this idea is the gypsies because we do not seek power over another. So, long before I was a vampire, I was and still am a gypsy, but with a path chosen by the stars. I must bring together the ones that we keepers call the prophecy's children. That includes you, my son."

Kabos placed a hand on Machiel's shoulder, and somehow that gave him a sense of peace. Machiel felt a little more confident in what lay before him despite the little nagging feeling of uncertainty, but he knew with Kabos at his side, things would turn out in the end. At least he hoped so. It was time to find this unusual river.

"My son, the road ahead of you is treacherous to fulfill this foretelling, but armed with the right ones to aid you, it will come to pass. I can read your thoughts, Machiel, and I feel the king inside you. He is silent, but he waits. Tell me more of what came to pass with you. I feel there is so much pain inside you."

Machiel and Kabos traveled by night and sought refuge from the sun for days. Machiel felt they were going in circles, not sure where to look. That's when the trees began to sway in the same direction, rustling their leaves, and the wind started to howl. The air became dense and a fog set in. The moon was not fully risen, but the night sky looked darker to Machiel than the previous nights of traveling. He began to wonder if they were getting closer or if they had gotten lost somehow.

Kabos lost his footing and tripped over a stone. Machiel reached for the old vampire and helped him along. As he looked up, his eyes became fixated on a small elfish-looking child. At least he presumed it was a child, though his eyes seemed rather dark and something about them gave him a weird sensation. Suddenly, he lost his grip on holding Kabos and his hands reached for his abdomen. The stone inside him gave him a sharp pain that just about crippled him to the ground. He could feel Kabos trying to help him stand, but he could not move. The only thing he could do was scream, and he did.

His eyes connected once more with the child. All he saw was the snarl on the child's face, and he heard the sound of laughter aimed at him. All Machiel could do at this point was look helplessly to Kabos. Before he could gain control of his body, the child disappeared. The pain stopped. But the pain reminded Machiel of his journey, and somehow, he cleared his mind and stood. Feeling renewed in the sense of purpose, Machiel held out his hand for Kabos, and the two continued to find their way. Inside, he felt the king stirring, though he remained silent. Machiel did not like this but fought his way through.

"Machiel, are you okay? What was that child?"

"I don't know, Father. But I felt like I knew him. When I get my talons on him, I'm going to shred his little body into millions of pieces. But remember me telling you about the stone, the one that hunter put in me? It was quiet, but not anymore. I think I can control the pain, but just know that it is constant. I feel it getting stronger. Maybe that means we are close. Who the hell knows what's what anymore? Father, I am so lost. I am nothing but a broken vampire."

Kabos urged Machiel to stop and rest. Pulling out an old parchment that resembled a map, Machiel and Kabos began to study it. From the looks of where they were and according to the ancient map, there should be a clearing ahead, but instead, there was nothing but trees and more forest. The night was getting darker, and the night animals were beginning to lurk in the dark.

Machiel was silent for a moment and then spoke. "Lady of the Prophecy, I beseech your wisdom. I do not mock you, but I do not know how to call for your aid. If I give myself to the prophecy and seek to do your justice, will you aid me and my father? Help me to remove this cursed stone from my gut."

Machiel could feel Kabos giving him a strange look—he didn't have to see him do it to know what he was doing. Machiel just shrugged as if to say it couldn't hurt to try to contact the prophecy. Kabos gave him a knowing look, but Machiel just shrugged again.

The two waited a bit longer to see what would happen. Nothing came. No one answered.

Machiel kicked his foot in the earth and was beginning to get annoyed. He began to feel afraid, but he was never afraid. Then he saw the child again, peering out from the woods, watching, and waiting. Machiel once more fell to the ground, doubling over in immense pain.

"Do you see him, Kabos? Over there. Just.... Oh, this damned stone! We must remove it."

Kabos ran to his son and tried to help him. "I see the child, Machiel. But look closer at his eyes. He is not a child. He is not even mortal, vampire, gypsy, witch, or wolf. We must hurry. My son, you do not see it, but the gypsy in me from long ago does. He is the one who controls the stone you carry inside. It is feeding off you to kill you, but not until you do its will. He is the one the prophecy warns us about. Think, Machiel! Think! What were you to do? There is no time. The king you speak of serves this child. But again, I tell you, this is no child. This is the form he takes, so people don't know he is pure evil."

Machiel couldn't remember the exact steps he was to do except find a cave—no, a river or two. His head was throbbing as he tried to remember.

Suddenly, calmness washed over him. The moon's silvery beam came down on Machiel, basking him in its light. Machiel felt free from the pain, from the hold of the stone and more. For once, he felt whole again. He stood erect. The pain had subsided. Machiel no longer felt the sharpness in his abdomen—the stone was silent once more. Machiel felt peace, as if the prophecy was with him, giving him aid. Was this what Beatrix had meant when she told him the prophecy would aid him in ways he would not understand? Looking in the direction of the child, he could see the child's eyes narrow, as if he, too, sensed the prophecy. Machiel just smiled like the victor he was toward the child, letting him know the prophecy had protected him. Pouting, the child turned on his heels and ran deeper into the forest, but not before dropping something. Machiel walked to pick it up and looked at it. It was nothing more than a strange piece of tree bark, all twisted and dead. Machiel discarded it without a second thought. He felt pure, in a way, knowing the prophecy protected him against this evil child.

Kabos stood next to Machiel and placed his hand on his shoulder. "Machiel, you are the one the prophecy needs. Serve her. Let's continue the

journey."
Machiel nodded.

CHAPTER 8

Machiel looked up at the moon and saw how bright it was. Looking at the forest ahead, it looked like nothing more than an endless maze. Though his body was feeling relief from the pain, he began to worry about this task before him.

Finally, he broke the silence between him and Kabos. "What is this stone of the damned? This thing inside me. I want it out, but what is it?"

"Ah, young vampire. Stories passed down between all the races, including ours, speak of this stone and others like it. You won't like hearing it—no one does. In fact, the story was used on me as a child to prevent the behaviors my parents did not like," he said jokingly. "I will try to remember. It's been so long, my son.

"Stories tell of four stones in total. Each resembles a cursed point. There is the stone of the damned, the stone of despair, the stone of hatred, and the stone of pride. Each stone was created in the image of the master, each with a common purpose. The master, in the beginning of time, sent the stones to his four most trusted servants. Each servant was to protect the stone so that when needed to be brought together, the master would always have his four stones and his four best servants to do his will. On our side, the side of the prophecy, each race—vampires, werewolves, witches, and gypsies—had what we referred to as a champion, if you will. That champion's calling was to seek the stones and take them into our keeping. This way, the master could not have them reunited.

"Before the prophecy spoke about a queen, there was another battle. The gypsies called it the Battle of the Beginning. We all fought together until the master rose from his depths with a fifth stone. This fifth stone, called the stone of the forsaken, was the most powerful stone anyone had seen. No one knew of its existence. Anyway, the master turned the tides on us all. He destroyed his own servants, the strongest we ever fought against, with this fifth stone. He destroyed the other stones, all save one. The one you carry inside you now.

"The stone of the damned is known to eat the wearer's soul and spirit while they are alive. Before the one who carries this stone realizes it, he no longer bends to his own will but to that of the master.

This Battle of the Beginning almost put us to extinction. We returned to our own parts of the world and tried to recover. Then the prophecy foretold of a queen. That provided our weakened selves the muster we needed to seek justice. The stone of the forsaken can be destroyed, but no one knows to this day how to do it. But this is the part of the vampire's story. I am sure that the witches, the gypsies and others have their own version. All we know is that it was lost, waiting to be found again. The vampires know nothing of how to destroy this stone, but in time, we might learn.

"Now, and quickly, we must remove that stone from you and destroy it."

Machiel, having listened carefully to this, became very somber and felt defeated. That was until he heard footsteps to the right. Having his guard up after experiencing all this led to his fangs emerging, his senses heightening. Smelling the air, he smelt the stench of a dire wolf. He recognized that canine smell in a second. But instead of the wolf, a six-foot man of solid build stood beside him and Kabos.

"Easy, friend. Put those fangs away. I am Killen, lord of my pack."

Kabos interjected before Machiel could make a move. "I am Kabos. This is Machiel. We have a mission. If I remember what Machiel said, there are two rivers that meet by a hidden cave. We are trying to find that cave. Are you familiar with this land?"

Holding his hands on his side, he began to laugh. "Do I know it, Kabos? Surely you jest." Killen laughed even harder. "You are in the land you seek. But, for the two rivers, that's a sad tale. The rivers dried up ages ago. Centuries ago, in fact. There is a cave, but no one has been in that cave for an eternity, it seems. Sometimes the children in our pack will play there, but not often. Do you want my assistance, lords of the night? I know of you, Kabos, the mystic one."

"What did you call us?" Machiel asked in return.

"Lords of the night. You are the blood drinkers, aren't you? You smell like them."

Kabos bowed.

"What are you doing, Father? Bowing to this dog?"

"No, Machiel. He is not a dog. He is a dire wolf, more ancient than the werewolves we know. More powerful, more legendary, if you will. Dire wolves are a special breed, special servants of the prophecy herself. We are below them, Machiel. Bow. Do it now. Don't be foolish. We are not above them at all.

There is still more for you to learn. I may have slipped in my teachings, my son."

Machiel, still not understanding, bowed to the man to his side. His sire commanded it, and thus he obeyed. But he did not like it one bit. He pulled back his fangs and relaxed his talons.

"May I, Machiel? Let me see what ails you. I will not harm you."

Machiel looked at Kabos, waiting. Kabos nodded his head.

Killen reached his hands towards Machiel's abdomen, and the moment became tense. Machiel always went by his instinctual behavior, and somehow, he seemed calm as Killen approached him. But this was not what he wanted. But perhaps this is what the prophecy wanted of him. Dire wolf, werewolf, it mattered not. He was going to let a mangy dog put their paws on him. Unbelievable! Machiel braced himself and used all his strength to control his anger and rage, minding what Kabos said. He, a vampire, was below a dire wolf.

Kabos broke the tension by asking, "Killen, may I ask you something?"

Killen replied, "Yes, lord."

"I know I am old, but it seems to me that it should be near morning, and we must seek shelter if you know what I mean. If the legends are true and the prophecy needs Machiel, then we must sleep."

There was a pause before Killen responded. "Lords of the night, you do not know everything, it seems. Or you must not have been told this part of the stories that hold true between the races. This land, this ground, is not affected by day or night. It is not a land to be controlled by either side. If your kind enters the land, then it will always be night. If one of those that walks during the day enters, then it will always be day. No one really knew where the Battle of the Beginnings took place, but it is believed to be here. Therefore, all are welcome and protected. Certain things can't be turned away from fate, however. So, Machiel. Please let me help you. I know what it is you seek and need. Hopefully, after this, you will consider my kind friend and not foe. We serve the prophecy and the side of right."

Machiel reluctantly gave in. He could feel Killen's hand on his abdomen. The stone inside him began to stir, causing little discomfort. Suddenly the stone started burning from the inside. Machiel screamed once more.

"By the stars! How did you get this inside you? Do you know what you have in you?"

Growling at Killen, in both pain and frustration, he said, "I have the stone of the damned in me, fool dog."

Killen explained how everyone knew this was the only surviving stone from that battle, but it had been lost. As Machiel listened, he remembered how Kabos said the same thing. The stone was lost. How it came to Machiel was still a wonder. More importantly, how could it be destroyed?

Killen stood and placed his forefinger and thumb together, whistling in the air. Trees began to move, and then Machiel saw it. The white wolf. She was a beautiful wolf, though a dog.

I have never seen a white wolf before. She doesn't even carry the wet stench of canine on her. She's so beautiful.

Machiel rubbed his eyes in disbelief. He found what he was seeking, but the stone brought him back to reality with another tinge of pain. Behind the wolf stood a woman. Just like the wolf, she, too, was beautiful.

"Machiel, child. I am glad to see you once more. This time, in my true form and not that of a child."

"My child, my Beatrix. Is she all right? And her mother? I must know that those I left behind are safe."

The woman smiled. "Yes, Machiel. All is what it should be. But it is you who are in most need right now. Come with me. Take my hand. Kabos, you come too."

Machiel and Kabos followed the woman, Killen, and the wolf deeper into the forest. Machiel noticed the child was watching them again.

CHAPTER 9

Machiel ignored what he saw and just kept moving. The group stopped periodically when he stumbled or fell because of the pain. Never, as a vampire, had he had streams of sweat running down his face. This was certainly a first. Stumbling again, Machiel finally collapsed to the ground, unconscious. He could hear them speaking but was not able to communicate back.

"Machiel, son. Wake up! Do something, Killen, please."

"Lord, it is not me who is doing this to him." Killen placed his hand over

Machiel's forehead. "He's burning. The stone is burning him from the inside. He's almost out of time."

Machiel's eyes fluttered open. "I'm so hot. The stone...the stone is...." His words stopped coming. Machiel closed his eyes once more and took a deep breath. He decided to use his mind to communicate with the woman and the wolf.

I am Machiel. Please tell me what to do. I don't know what's worse, this burning or when the hunter played games with my body. I won't forsake the prophecy again. I beg for forgiveness but seek your aid. Please help me.

The wolf spoke back with her mind. *Child. Listen to me. To free yourself from the stone, you must allow me to bite you. It will not kill you. Once I bite you, you will sleep. For how long is up to you. While you sleep, you will be sent on a quest. This is not my choosing. On this quest, you must decide. You will listen. You will choose. This is the only way.*

Machiel agreed to this through his mind. He wished he could tell the others, but something inside him told him he couldn't. While he spoke to the wolf with his mind, the stone's grip on him got tighter. It was almost like the stone and the wolf were pulling at him from different directions. It was a battle that Machiel wasn't sure he would survive. At least that's what it felt like. Machiel opened his eyes once more and smiled.

"Do your will."

Before anyone could respond or question his words, the white wolf leaped into the air and landed on all fours, right on top of Machiel's chest. Snarling with her teeth, the drool began to drop onto Machiel's neck. Within mere seconds, the white wolf changed position and ripped into his abdomen, tearing away the skin and exposing the stone. The stone was a shade of grey with red lines staggered, with no sense of a pattern. It was triangular in shape with a small hole on one side, allowing Machiel's intestines to latch themselves onto it.

Gasps of horror filled the night as the stone began to darken to black. Machiel's body was holding onto the stone, and the wolf was trying to tear it away. She tried to rip into an intestine, but that only caused Machiel to scream louder than before. His screams pierced the silence of the night, and his eyes remained open, fully aware of what was transpiring.

Kabos was yelling that the wolf was killing him. The woman responded kindly that the decision was Machiel's, and he must go through this. The stone's hold on Machiel, she explained, was the doing of the master. The wolf pulled, the stone held tighter. It was never-ending.

"Sit, while we wait. Let me tell you what I saw in Machiel's when I met him through his daughter. Machiel was tormented at the hands of the hunter. He was conflicted — still is. He senses and understands his duty to the prophecy and to the queen, but an agreement was made between the king and the hunter, both servants of the master. The master has many names, many faces. The agreement was that Machiel would serve as host to the king when the coming battle happens. The stone of the damned is his way to control Machiel and remind him of his other purpose. The king has returned and lives in Machiel. They are one, in a way. As you can see, Machiel is conflicted. The wolf will not harm him, but her bite is known to put her victims on a quest — a self journey to see the truth and find purpose.

"The white wolf and I serve the prophecy, not the master or the true one. Machiel's quest is his and his alone. When he awakens, the quest will be done. His answer will determine his fate."

Killen and Kabos looked into Machiel's eyes, and he couldn't speak to them. He could see them, but he couldn't reassure him that this was to be. He felt remorse for his past actions, but as the wolf kept biting into him, he remained in his trance-like state, unable to speak or move. Finally, he closed his eyes with the final bite. He felt the wolf move off him, freeing his body from the weight.

Machiel began his quest. He could see images from the past and was only witnessing what must have transpired then. He could make out images of the bloodiest battle amongst the races and what looked to be this master. The master was not man, vampire, or wolf. He was simply demonic. Next to him sat a hunter — not Valentine, but similar. On the other side was a young woman bound by a collar and chains.

The images changed. He saw the master giving four servants a stone each. Then he saw the one that was placed inside him. It was given to a servant that had a familiar face, but he couldn't quite make out who it was. Again the images changed. Now he saw a battle being fought, races united and fighting together. Werewolves and vampires together? It couldn't be. But what could've changed it to where the dogs served the vampires now? The master looked defeated and grabbed the same girl by the chain and hoisted her above him. Laughing, he threw her into a pit of fire. Machiel cringed at the sight.

Machiel took a deep breath. He

thought to himself that these images meant something, but what? He continued to see more. He saw her again, another image of the woman consorting with the wolf and a king watching them. She, too, was eventually killed. *What the hell is it with killing women?* Machiel continued his quest. This time there were no images but a long path for him to follow. He started walking.

As he walked closer to the end of the path, he realized he couldn't feel the stone anymore. In fact, he touched his abdomen to see if it was still there. It was. He felt a strong force pulling him closer to the door that lay at the end of the path. Touching the door, he began to feel around for a way to open it. He accidentally rested his hand against the door, and it started to move. Pushing his way through the door was easy as if the door was expecting him—but that was ridiculous. He moved inside the room, and there was nothing there—just an empty black space.

Growing more curious, Machiel yelled out to the darkness. "It is I, Machiel. Do you know who I am?"

Silence filled his ears. No sounds, no movement, nothing but the darkness. Suddenly he saw the white witch, more beautiful than he could imagine.

"Machiel, you must choose. You left the prophecy out of anger. You came back to it out of love for your child. You can choose left, you can choose right, but only you can choose. See the two stones that lay on the table over there?"

Just like with everything else, a table just appeared with two stones. Machiel nodded to the white witch.

"Each stone represents a path. You don't know which path it is meant for. Before you just grab a stone from the table, I want you to reach inside yourself. I want you to feel the stone of the damned. Do you feel its hold on you?"

"Yes. I feel it. I feel weak when it burns me. It hurts."

"That's the stone feeding off you. I can't change that. But I can help you choose how to live with it inside you or teach you how to remove it. That's part of your destiny, Machiel. The fates have spoken about a young vampire, torn between two worlds. He will wear two faces but, in the end, his true face will emerge. You are the young vampire, but your destiny is complex. Can you handle the stone of the damned in you, or do you want to remove it?"

"If I remove it, what will happen to it? If I think like Kabos, he would worry about the stone and whose hands it would fall into. If I think like me, I would want it gone from my body. I never asked for such a burden, but I understand the needs. The needs of the many sometimes outweigh the needs of the one, says Kabos. I need time."

"Machiel, this place is free of time and space. Think on it. The stone's hold on you is paused while you remain in this room. But know that anyone can come in this room whose fate is tied to yours. So beware, young vampire. This room is a place for both friend and foe of the prophecy. It is a sanctuary but at a price." And with that, she disappeared.

Machiel paced the floor, touching his abdomen every once in a while. Not knowing much about women, he began to chuckle that he was touching his abdomen like a woman touches her belly to feel her unborn child. He thought he was alone, but he wasn't—the child entered the room. Machiel heard his tiny footsteps, and using his agility, he was face to face with this demon child, or whatever it was.

"Machiel, you are much younger than I thought you would be. But I can see you will do nicely. I need you to hand me the stone. Serve me and no other. I can free you from all that you do not want and reward you with riches."

Machiel refused. Instead, he bared his fangs and hissed at the child. He'd never killed a child before, but something inside told him this would be different. The child did not even flinch. Instead, he raised his arm till it was even with his torso and extended his hand, palm open. The child closed his eyes, and before Machiel could do anything, the child turned into a goat. Then he turned into a man before becoming a child once more. The child kept changing shapes as if he was taunting Machiel, but he stood fast against this evil.

"What are you?"

The child laughed. "I am many things, Machiel. But you can call me Sammael. I think you and I could do great things together if you just give yourself to me. I know you have the missing stone — the stone of the damned — inside you. I can feel it. I need that stone to be in my possession once more. You do not know how to control it. But I do. You see, it once belonged to me a very long time ago. I know the king lives in you. This is good. It's a start."

Machiel felt tormented by the immense feelings of confusion. Kneeling on the ground, he cupped his hands over his ears and screamed. Suddenly, the stone inside him became alive once more. Machiel and the stone were becoming one. A few moments later, he ran to where the two small stones lay. He stared at them. How to choose?

Machiel closed his eyes once more. He felt the power of those closest to him. Perhaps Killen was going to be a friend, after all. Perhaps the white witch was right. Perhaps this child was right. He didn't feel the sense of the prophecy, so that told him it was all up to him to choose. *Do I just take a stone?* Not wanting to feel defeated once more, Machiel walked away from the table.

He shouted to the room, hoping somebody or something would hear his cry.

"I will keep the stone inside me — I will control its power. I will honor Kabos in choosing to believe in the prophecy. I will be its instrument."

The child screamed, and the walls of the room began to shake. Machiel, believing he would be crushed, tried to close his eyes but found that they would not close. He could not move. The room was not closing in as he thought based on the shaking he felt. Instead, he saw the white witch again. This time she was with the white wolf. It was beginning to make sense. The white witch and the white wolf were actually one but could appear in two forms.

"Machiel, you have made your choice, but I see you did not choose a stone. Why is that?"

"If I chose a stone, you will know what stone was chosen. If I leave both on the table, then I still have some control in my choice. Teach me to control the stone of the damned, so it can remain protected."

The white wolf came forward and eventually transformed into another woman, just as beautiful and identical to the white witch. From her hand, she gave him a berry to eat.

"Eat this and become one with the

stone."

Machiel ate the berry but didn't feel any different than he had moments before. After some minutes, Machiel began to twitch. Suddenly, he leaned forward and vomited. The stone was now on the floor, along with some bodily fluids. Disgusted, he reached for the stone, expecting it to burn him, but it didn't.

"Go ahead, pick it up. The stone belongs to you now — you are connected to it. But take heed…it still yearns for its original master. But you control it. It is part of you, just like the king is. You can control all if you have patience. If you lose the stone, the master can find it. Once united with the stone of the forsaken, a new hell will be unleashed to the world, and that would be a grave mistake, Machiel. Do you wish to continue your choice?"

A little afraid of his choice, he muttered yes.

"Machiel, do not fear the prophecy. Listen to Kabos, to your teachings. Study the legends; hide the stone; learn the ways of everything you can. For when you are needed, you will know. You will know when you meet her. Till then, prepare the way.

"You can control the stone by holding it and whispering the words we will teach you. But know the stone also has a mind of its own and may resist. It is still one of the master's stones from long before. If you lose it, and it somehow ends up in the hands of the master, know that the world will face an unspeakable horror. Because you have the stone, you have the choice. But know you are never alone and never will be. Learn what you can about the history of battles, the stones, the prophecy, from all those that will teach you. Curb your anger for those not of the vampire race. Unite with all, become one with all in order to remain in control. Allies can prove to be the greatest force against the master and his evil servants."

Machiel learned the words and a little more about his destiny, promising not to reveal all. He also learned that Killen was a trusted man and a comrade. Should he ever need the dire wolves, they would come. A new alliance was made. Dire wolves would come in this century or the next, whenever Machiel had a need. Once the instruction was done, the path appeared once more, and Machiel followed it to return.

CHAPTER 10

Machiel awoke from his trance and saw he was surrounded by those who had stayed by his side. He saw Kabos, Killen, the white witch, and the white wolf. He tried to sit up, but gentle hands kept him down, urging him to rest. Machiel lifted up his hands for everyone to see. He carried with him the stone of the damned. Kabos reached to touch it, but as his finger barely touched it, it shot a bolt of energy, sending Kabos flying through the air.

Machiel called for Kabos. "Father! Father!"

"I am fine, son. But the stone…it seems no one can touch it but you. What does this mean?"

Machiel sat up eventually and began to tell everyone about the quest and how the stone came to be his. Everyone listened, and slowly, it was no longer just the five of them. Dire wolves came out and sat all around them, listening and looking at the stone of the damned.

Killen spoke. "Machiel, you are brave, my young vampire friend. This is my pack. We will come to your aid when needed. We are now allies. We consider you family. Stay with us for a while if you can. Let us teach you and Kabos some of our ways and add to your knowledge of the prophecy, if you let us."

Machiel looked at Kabos and shrugged. Kabos, not saying a word, just nodded, and elation filled the forest. Kabos wanted to know more about the stone of the damned, the cursed thing. Machiel did his best to tell them everything he could, leaving out the parts he was sworn to secrecy about. Machiel was not tired, but he could feel that he no longer had a sense of time in this forest. He liked that. It was peaceful. They needed to feed, but a wolf child brought them some animals, explaining that it was all they had.

"Thank you, child. What is your name?"

"I am Jens. You are my first vampire I ever did meet," said the young wolf child.

Killen invited them all to celebrate in their new beginnings. "Tomorrow is a big day — lots of schooling for Machiel and Kabos. Let's feast and sleep. Tomorrow will be here faster than we realize."

After a good rest, Machiel and Kabos found themselves in school.

Machiel remembered always being a good student, though mischievous. Somehow that had never grown out of his nature, as he tried to make the children laugh at his antics. Kabos kept nudging him in the side and motioning for him to remain silent. Killen's wife was the teacher, and these children were learning their history as well as the history of the other races. Fascinated by the way the prophecy was so complex and so simple at the same time, Machiel finally quieted down.

Machiel gave it good thought. There was a battle in the beginning — the master was defeated. And now, there was supposed to be another battle, this time involving a queen. Machiel scratched his head as he listened to the legends about the gypsies. This was Kabos's kind before he became a vampire, full of seers and swordsmen. It seemed like the gypsies were also a kind of keeper of the prophecy. But the one race that really intrigued him was the witches, hundreds of covens of witches. His mind was spinning.

Killen's wife was telling the history of the witches and the Tall Dark Man. This time he really sat still to listen.

"The Tall Dark Man—no one knows his true name or nature—appears in many different forms. But you can recognize him by his eyes. He has brown eyes, but not like the normal brown eyes you see in others. His brown eyes have an empty look about them. He can be a child, he can be a man, he can be a goat. But he usually takes one of these three forms. He is attracted to witches because of their power and their line. He can spread his seed through the witches and cultivate them into his power. This makes them the easiest of all prey.

"If you come across the Tall Dark Man, know it was no mistake. Witches become trapped to his every wish, his every command. Through them, his numbers grow. Some of the most powerful witches cannot resist his traps. Witches have been around as long as any of the races, except for our kind. We, the dire wolves, are the ancient ones. Witches, vampires, werewolves — they all have a stake in the prophecy. Separated, they will not win, but together, they stand a chance."

Machiel remembered something from his quest. It was a part of his quest that didn't need to remain a secret. Machiel cleared his throat so that he could speak.

" The Tall Dark Man, as you call him. The child, the goat, the man. He has a name. He told it to me during my quest. His name is Sammael."

Machiel and Kabos could hear everyone gasp, and this bit of news must be shared.

"Are you sure that's what he said, Machiel? If you are certain, we must get word of his true name to all the races so that it can be recorded and made known. You never know when it might be needed in order to defeat him."

Machiel nodded, and upon doing so, Killen ran to one of the fast wolves and told him to bring the message to the other races. Inform all about the name Sammael. After doing so, Killen turned to face Machiel and nodded in gratitude.

A cold wind blew through the forest, and the white wolf appeared. She howled at the night sky as if to warn the pack of a threat looming about. Machiel's ears perked up, and he listened for anything that seemed out of the ordinary.

Machiel, follow me. Bring Kabos.

Machiel reached for Kabos and signaled for him to follow the white wolf. Leaving the pack behind them, the wolf showed them what was of concern. There she lay against the ground, her body cold and frigid — it was the white witch. Her body was badly bruised and broken, her white hair tangled with specks of dirt. In her hands, she held a piece of parchment. She must have torn it from the attacker.

Kabos screamed, but not loudly enough to strike panic in the children. Machiel said, "No! Not her. Why?"

The white wolf changed her shape to the one Machiel had met while on his quest. "Machiel, child. The Tall Dark Man presented himself to you, did he not? In the form of a child?"

"Yes. He offered me a way to join him, but I refused. He wants his stone, doesn't he?"

"I was afraid of this. You are safe

here if you stay with the dire wolves, but the stone is not. It knows its true master is also here."

The white wolf-woman approached the white witch and took the parchment from her hand. As she did, she noticed that underneath the body was a book. She must have been protecting that book and died because of it. She took the book and walked towards Machiel and Kabos.

"Look what she was protecting. I have never seen this before."

The trio looked at the worn cover of the book. Then Machiel noticed the title. He recognized the language, but it was one that was being taught to him by Kabos. He was not quite an expert in it.

"Kabos, it's in the language of the gypsies. Look."

"Yes, my dear boy. So it seems. Let me see the book, please."

The book was handed to Kabos,

and he began to open it, being careful of its pages. Then he saw the part where the page was torn. He asked for the torn piece and tried to read aloud the pages around the missing part. Machiel watched Kabos's face and noticed it change to somber.

"Kabos, what is it? Tell us, please! Is there something at stake with us all?" questioned the white wolf-woman. She appeared to be getting quite anxious with this new book being found.

"I don't believe it. The things I was taught as a child and what I keep learning now are different than this book. The first sentence reads, 'This is the original story of the stars and the prophecy to be.' And then it goes on and on. This is written in the old tongue, and it matches the scrolls from Eshmun in my collection. We must guard this book and the stone. I feel they are connected to all of this. We cannot let this fall into the hands of the Tall Dark Man or any other non-believers. White wolf, what is your name so I may properly address you?"

"It is Keela. The white witch was my sister Kala. We were two halves of a whole. But we help to guard the prophecy and those that follow it. We lead the way, but their destiny is not something we can control. But, if you feel you can guard the book and the stone, do so. It will require you to leave here because I can't let anything happen to the dire wolves. Machiel, are you ready without more training, more assistance? Kabos may be older and wiser, but you are the one meant to find the queen. You will have no protection once you leave this forest."

Machiel smiled, but deep down, he knew he was terrified. He looked at the stone he never let go of and the book. Kabos said he was destined for a higher purpose, so he might as well obey the prophecy. After all, he had made his choice on his quest. Machiel could only nod and took the book from Kabos. Both items were now in his safekeeping.

"How long do we have before we really have to leave the forest?"

"It is best to go as soon as possible, dear Kabos and Machiel. Heed these words. Use the time given to you wisely. The queen won't come until it's her time. Till she has learned what will be needed to succeed. Machiel, arm yourself with friends from all races and learn all languages, including the languages that seem lost, like this book. Collect the knowledge—study the prophecy from all angles. Do not forsake your destiny. Use everything to your advantage to become formidable. That is the best I can offer you, in addition to providing you these amulets. These amulets will only mask the book and stone for thirty-six moons to allow you safe passage to hide them until time calls for them. The dire wolves have already prepared baskets of fresh blood to sustain you, and the forest will hide you from the sun until you reach Italy. You must go to Italy, and from there, make your way to your people, Kabos, to the gypsies. Fare thee well, sons."

Machiel and Kabos rejoined the others and accepted a special blue cloth to wrap the book in to protect it from the weather while on their journey. It was a midnight blue cloth, laced with gold tassels on each corner. Wrapping the book ever so gently, Machiel noticed the gold triangle with the eye in the middle. He also wrapped the stone with the book because, as they had witnessed before, no one but Machiel could touch it. Killen's wife handed Kabos the basket, and the smell of fresh blood made Machiel divert his attention from the book. His fangs protruded, and it startled the children, but once he noticed their fear, he gained control and resisted that sweet aroma.

Machiel and Kabos began their journey with the amulets around their necks. He was a little more confident in his choice now than before but still fearful of what he must learn.

CHAPTER 11

Once they arrived in Italy, Kabos made arrangements for services they would need. He had hired dispatchers to run errands during the day and a housekeeper that enjoyed cleaning at night while they hunted and secreted themselves away to read. Machiel felt like he was learning nothing but ancient languages, but he'd made a promise to Keela.

He studied the prophecy and learned that the different races had so many versions. The vampire prophecy seemed to be a bit more two-sided, in his opinion. On one hand, the werewolves were to be servants, yet on the other, according to the ancient book they were studying, united races were more important. Machiel seemed to be conflicted again based on the vampire prophecy, his prophecy. Kabos tried to explain, but it was just as confusing.

"Kabos, I don't understand. If the queen is the one to unite the races, then why do the vampires teach us about the werewolves not being equal? We met the dire wolves, and Killen was actually friendly. I just don't understand it."

"Machiel, when you are ready, I will teach you about our laws in more detail. First, let's get through this book and what the original stars want to tell us. It seems to be a rather big book to read in just one sitting. Perhaps that's why they gave us so much time that the book will be protected. To read it and learn it before hiding it. Do you still have the stone?"

"Yes, Father. The stone never leaves my possession. Let's eat and then continue with the book. We just have a few hours left before the sun comes up."

Kabos flipped through the pages gently and came upon a passage. This was about the first battle, The Battle of the Beginnings. "Machiel, listen to this. It's about the Battle of the Beginnings."

Machiel sat next to Kabos and listened as Kabos started to read, summarizing the best he could from the old language.

"The Battle of the Beginnings was the first battle between the sides. It involved all races of supernatural birth. The master called forth his four servants and provided them with speed, strength, and a stone each. Each servant scattered to the ends of the earth, separated but hidden until the master would send word for the stones' need. Each stone remained dormant but alive, waiting for the master to call it home. The vampires found the first servant and destroyed both him and the stone. The werewolves found the second servant and destroyed them both. The third servant and stone were destroyed by the witches. The fourth servant lost his life to the gypsies, and though it was in their possession at one point, it was soon lost, never to be seen again. All the races searched for this stone–the stone of the damned–but it never turned up until now. The master received news about his servants' demise via their severed heads, which were sent back to him in blue satchels, each marked with the symbol of each race.

"Because of this, the master created a fifth stone. The stone of the forsaken. This stone is known to open the gateway that will unleash the most powerful demonic form ever created. The stone was created from what we refer to as 'fire rock that flows.' This demon will have the might and power to destroy everything in its path, friend or foe if ever released. It is said that if the stone of the forsaken is united with the stone of the damned, the other stones, if destroyed, will form once more. Another battle involving a queen will prepare the races for reunification. Once that battle has been decided, the world will prepare again—this time for a third battle.

"Machiel, I don't believe it. There are to be three battles. One in the beginning, the one with the queen, and then a third battle. Three battles. Each battle represents the three sisters of fate. The first sister of fate is the keeper of the first battle. The second sister is the keeper of the second battle. The last sister is the keeper of the third battle. Once the three battles for the sisters are completed — no mention which side has to be victorious — the sisters of fate will destroy the stone of the forsaken and put the master in chains, or something like that. Oh, Machiel, we have to prepare, and I must get word dispatched to the other races."

Machiel couldn't fathom what he'd heard. His mind was racing once more from the telling of the prophecy. He remembered what Keela and Kala had tried to teach him on his quest. Patience, virtue, alliances. Three of the many things he was going to need to succeed. He didn't move for some time, but finally, he spoke.

"Kabos, three sisters of fate? Three battles? There's more to come to unite the races? What am I going to do?"

Machiel started to tremble as

he'd never experienced a battle, but just thinking about the Battle of the Beginnings scared him to death. And now he was to be part of the second battle. Fear encompassed him but slowly transformed to rage. He slammed his hand down on the ledge and screamed into the night air. He felt the stone come to life in his pocket. His abdomen started to burn, but not painfully. Just enough to make him realize the true nature of his destiny and what he had committed to.

"Kabos, we can do this. But you need to teach me everything you know. And I need to become one with the prophecy and this stone. I think there is more to the stone than we know. Perhaps we can use it. Does the book say anything more about the stone of the damned since the others were destroyed?"

Kabos flipped through the pages again. He came across a section about the four stones.

"Here we are. The four stones. The stone of the damned, the stone of despair, the stone of hatred, and the stone of pride. Together, these stones will make the four holders act as one. Separately, they serve no purpose, but it seems that the stone of the damned has the power to not just bend the holder to the will of the master but to bring back the other stones. With the four stones and the stone of the forsaken, they will find their way to the master, and once that is done, all is lost. The sisters of fate will lose the power of foretelling."

Kabos paused for a moment before continuing. "We can't let any of this happen, Machiel. We must prepare you. We must give you knowledge and power, not just in you but in your alliances. Let's return to the house."

Once they returned, they found

the housekeeper busily working, and she smiled as they walked into the hall.

"Sweet Greta, I must find my dispatchers. Please find them and tell them there will be letters of importance on the desk in the study for them, along with directions. They should prepare to be away for some time to see these messages are delivered where they need to go. My son and I must tend to other matters now. Thank you, sweet Greta. You are a gem."

"Sir Kabos, I am at your service."

Kabos and Machiel prepared the letters, and Machiel wrote exactly what Kabos told him to. These letters were sent to each of the races, to the dire wolves, and to the Avalani. The time to prepare for what was yet to come was at hand. Machiel could feel the stone, and somehow he knew it was time to learn more about the stone than what was in this book.

He left Kabos in the study and went to another room in the house. He found a quiet place to write a letter to Rosalia. Knowing her story helped him ask for help. In that letter, he explained about what he had learned, not revealing his whereabouts, and he asked for help. In the end of the letter, he asked about his precious daughter and hoped that both were still safe. He brought the letter back and put it in the stack for the dispatchers, hoping Kabos would not notice.

Now to exercise patience as he waited for the reply. Feeling drained from all the events that had kept him busy, Machiel retired and simply slept. The next night would begin the next part of the training and preparation, but for now, at least, he had Kabos at his side and new alliances to be made. The second battle would come, but no one knew when. Thus, began the years of preparation that lay in store for Machiel. His life was no longer his — it belonged to the prophecy he served.

I was born in Hawaii, a place rich with culture and storytellers. As a little girl, scary tales about vampires, werewolves, angels, demons, and witches were my favorite kind— much to my mother's dismay.

The scarier, the better.

My love for the supernatural never went away, even after moving to Seattle, far from Hawaii's majestic beaches with unusual colors. Nothing compares to the landscapes of Maui, Lanai, or Oahu. But somehow, Seattle stole my heart anyway. It became the place where my love for stories took on a new form, in a book of my own: The Adventures of Little Arthur and Merlin the Magnificent. This book is for kids who love stories, just like I did.

Then I had an idea while sleeping.

One night, my mind began to work overtime. In a dream, I saw a unique storyline involving all the races and an epic battle of good versus evil. It was a modern-day plot with a three thousand year old prophecy, The Blood Prophecy. I finished the first book in 2014, The Queen's Destiny. Two years later, I released The Queen's Enemy. The last book in the series, The Queen's Ascension, arrives this Spring 2020.

Today, I live in Florida with its beaches

and sunshine. But I'm still a Seattle girl at heart. And so all my stories take place in the Northwest.

I always keep to my roots when I write.

- Barb Jones